MID-CONTINENT PUBLIC LIBRARY
15616 E. 24 HWY
INDEPENDENCE, MO 64050

3 0 0 0 4 0 0 0 9 4 1

D0367001

WELCOME TO
PASSPORT TO READING
A beginning reader's ticket to a brand-new world!

Every book in this program is designed to build read-along and read-alone skills, level by level, through engaging and enriching stories. As the reader turns each page, he or she will become more confident with new vocabulary, sight words, and comprehension.

These PASSPORT TO READING levels will help you choose the perfect book for every reader.

READING TOGETHER
Read short words in simple sentence structures together to begin a reader's journey.

READING OUT LOUD
Encourage developing readers to sound out words in more complex stories with simple vocabulary.

READING INDEPENDENTLY
Newly independent readers gain confidence reading more complex sentences with higher word counts.

READY TO READ MORE
Readers prepare for chapter books with fewer illustrations and longer paragraphs.

This book features sight words from the educator-supported Dolch Sight Words List. This encourages the reader to recognize commonly used vocabulary words, increasing reading speed and fluency.

For more information, please visit passporttoreadingbooks.com.

Enjoy the journey!

Copyright © 2015 Disney Enterprises, Inc. All rights reserved.
Cover © 2015 Disney Enterprises, Inc. All rights reserved.
Cover design by Bobby Lopez
Cover art by the Disney Storybook Art Team

In accordance with the U.S. Copyright Act of 1976, the scanning, uploading, and electronic sharing of any part of this book without the permission of the publisher is unlawful piracy and theft of the author's intellectual property. If you would like to use material from the book (other than for review purposes), prior written permission must be obtained by contacting the publisher at permissions@hbgusa.com. Thank you for your support of the author's rights.

Little, Brown and Company

Hachette Book Group
1290 Avenue of the Americas, New York, NY 10104
Visit us at lb-kids.com

Little, Brown and Company is a division of Hachette Book Group, Inc. The Little, Brown name and logo are trademarks of Hachette Book Group, Inc.

The publisher is not responsible for websites (or their content) that are not owned by the publisher.

First Edition: February 2015

Library of Congress Control Number: 2014953023

ISBN 978-0-316-28350-2

10 9 8 7 6 5 4 3 2 1

CW

Printed in the United States of America

Passport to Reading titles are leveled by independent reviewers applying the standards developed by Irene Fountas and Gay Su Pinnell in *Matching Books to Readers: Using Leveled Books in Guided Reading*, Heinemann, 1999.

Meet Fawn
the Animal-Talent Fairy

By Jennifer Fox

Illustrated by the Disney Storybook Art Team

LITTLE, BROWN AND COMPANY
New York • Boston

Attention, Disney Fairies fans!
Look for these words when you read
this book. Can you spot them all?

hawk

comet

rocks

storm

Fawn loves animals
with all her heart.

She wants to
help every critter
in the forest.

Fawn will even help out a baby hawk.

"Hawks eat fairies!"

Tink warns.

Fawn tells Tink that is not true.

Fawn fixes the hawk's wing.

"Hawk!" an animal fairy shouts.

Three new hawks fly in.

"Everyone, get inside," a fairy says.

Everyone is scared.

A scout fairy gets the
baby hawk under a net.

Queen Clarion says
Fawn should not bring
dangerous animals into
Pixie Hollow.

Fawn tries very hard
to follow this rule.

Yet when she hears a roar

in the forest, she follows

a trail of paw prints.

She finds a big and scary creature.

He is also fluffy.

"Hey, big guy," says Fawn.

"What are you?"

He is a NeverBeast.

The NeverBeast was

asleep for many years.

Then a comet woke him up.

Fawn decides to be his friend.

She names him Gruff and

helps him with his hurt paw.

Gruff builds towers of rocks.

Fawn adds a few.

"Now we are talking," she says.

Back home,
the scout fairies find
signs of the NeverBeast.
They find a trail and
bite marks.

They think a dangerous
animal is in Pixie Hollow!

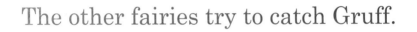

The other fairies try to catch Gruff.

"Follow me,"
Fawn says to Gruff.
She knows in her
heart that he is good.
She will prove it
to the fairies.

A big storm comes.

It lights up the sky.

Fawn shows the others

how Gruff protects them.

He blocks the lightning.

Gruff's job is done.

He is tired,

but Pixie Hollow is safe.

The fairies walk him

back to his cave.

Gruff rests his head
on a pillow.
It is time for him
to go back to sleep.
"I love you, Gruff!"
says Fawn.

The big furry beast will
always hold a special
place in her heart.